This book belongs to

. . . .

LADYBIRD BOOKS

UK | USA | Canada | Ireland | Australia | India | New Zealand | South Africa

Ladybird Books is part of the Penguin Random House group of companies
whose addresses can be found at global.penguinrandomhouse.com.

www.penguin.co.uk   www.puffin.co.uk   www.ladybird.co.uk

Penguin
Random House
UK

First published 2018
002

Printed in China

A CIP catalogue record for this book is available from the British Library

ISBN: 978-0-241-32153-9

All correspondence to:
Ladybird Books
Penguin Random House Children's
80 Strand, London WC2R 0RL

Peppa Meets Father Christmas

It was almost Christmas. Peppa was wrapped up
in her warm winter clothes and on her way
to playgroup.
"I can't wait for Christmas Day!" cried Peppa,
as she and George jumped up
and
down in the snow.

Snort!

Ho! Ho! Ho!

"Has everyone got their costumes for the Christmas play?" asked Madame Gazelle, once everyone had arrived. Peppa and her friends all had parts to practise for the play.

Hooray!

"Ho! Ho! Ho!" barked Danny Dog. Danny was Father Christmas.
"I'm the Christmas Fairy!" said Peppa, dancing around proudly.
"I'm the Christmas nurse," said Suzy, "in case anybody gets ill."

The next day, Peppa, George, Mummy and Daddy Pig
went to the supermarket to do some Christmas shopping.

"Daddy, look!" whispered Peppa, pointing. "It's Father Christmas!"
"Why don't you go over and say hello?" said Daddy Pig.

"Hello, Father Christmas," said Peppa shyly. "It's me, Peppa."

"Hello, Peppa," Father Christmas replied. "Are you looking forward to Christmas?"

"Oooh, yes!" said Peppa. "We're doing a Christmas play at playgroup. I'm the Christmas Fairy and Danny is you." "How lovely!" said Father Christmas.

"I should be Father Christmas, really," said Peppa. "But Danny is good at *Ho-ho-ho*-ing!"

"Ho! Ho! Ho!" laughed Father Christmas.

"Will you come and see our play?" asked Peppa. "Pleeeaase!"

"I am rather busy," Father Christmas replied, "but I will do my best!"

At playgroup the next day, Peppa and her friends put up the Christmas tree.

"I saw Father Christmas at the supermarket!" cried Peppa. "He's coming to see our play!" "I saw him at the garden centre and he didn't tell me that," said Rebecca Rabbit.

"I saw Father Christmas in the shopping centre," said Molly Mole. "How can he be in so many places?"

"Father Christmas moves very quickly," said Danny Dog. "He gives presents to children all around the world in just one night."

"On his magic sleigh!" added Zoe Zebra,
putting the last decoration on the tree.

The next morning, Peppa saw Father Christmas
at the Christmas-tree shop.
"Hello again, Father Christmas!" cried Peppa.
"Are you still coming to our play?"

"Play?" asked Father Christmas.

"Our Christmas play!" said Peppa. "You haven't forgotten?"

"Oh yes, of course. I will do my best to come," replied Father Christmas.

The day of the Christmas play arrived.
"We can't start yet," whispered Peppa.
"Father Christmas isn't here."
"But your parents are waiting," whispered
Madame Gazelle. "The show must go on!"

The snowflakes started the play with a song.
"*Snow, snow – it's what we like.*
Snow by day, and snow by night.
And when it falls it turns things white.
Snow, snow, snow!"

"I am the Christmas Fairy!" said Peppa, jumping on stage.
"And I am Father Christmas," said Danny Dog, joining her.
"Ho! Ho! Ho! WOOF!"

"Ho! Ho! Ho!

"Ho! Ho! Ho! Wonderful!" said a voice.
It sounded just like . . .
"Father Christmas!" gasped the children. "You're here!"

"You came to see our play after all!" cried Peppa.
"Of course I did, Peppa," said Father Christmas. "It's very good."

"Do you really go all around the world in one night?" asked Wendy Wolf.
"Yes," replied Father Christmas. "With my magic sleigh and reindeer."

"Please can we see your sleigh?" asked Pedro Pony.
"I'm sure Father Christmas is a bit too busy to show
us his sleigh," said Madame Gazelle.

"It's true, I am VERY busy. But of course you can see my sleigh," said Father Christmas. "Come outside, everyone."

Father Christmas led the children, their families and Madame Gazelle outside.

"Wow!" everyone gasped, seeing his golden sleigh sparkling in the snow.
"It's beautiful!" cried Peppa. "What is it like to ride in?"
"Hop in, and I'll show you," replied Father Christmas.

"Whoooo!" cried the children,
as Father Christmas flew them across the sky.
"Ho! Ho! Ho!" laughed Father Christmas.
"Happy Christmas, everyone!"

Ho! Ho! Ho!

"This is the best Christmas ever!"
cheered Peppa. "Thank you, Father Christmas!"

Merry Christmas!